and also to

....

....

For you both with my love

William Collins Sons & Co Ltd
London · Glasgow · Sydney · Auckland
Toronto · Johannesburg

First published 1989
© Text Bryan Forbes Ltd 1989
© Illustrations Liz Moyes 1989

A CIP catalogue record for this book is available
from the British Library

ISBN 0 00 184574 8

Printed in Great Britain
by William Collins Sons & Co Ltd, Glasgow

Sharing

NANETTE NEWMAN
Illustrated by Liz Moyes

Collins

"Do you know what," said Indie's Mummy.

"What?" said Indie.

"I've got a baby in my tummy."

"Why?" said Indie.

"Well," said her Mummy, "I thought it would be nice for you to have a brother or a sister."

Indie thought for a minute.

"Could you have a dog instead?" she asked.

"Now don't be silly," said her Mummy. "Would you like to feel it?"

Indie put her hands on her Mummy's tummy.

"There – did you feel it kick?" said her Mummy.

"Why don't you give it a smack?" said Indie.

Her Mummy pulled down her sweater and told Indie it was time to go to the park.

Indie sat in the sandpit with her friend Cleo.

"My Mummy's got a baby in her tummy," said Indie.

"Oh," said Cleo. "When will it come out?"

"When it feels like it," said Indie.

"Will it be a boy baby or a girl?" asked Cleo.

"No one knows," said Indie.

"Do you wish it was a dog?" asked Cleo.

"Yes," said Indie.

The time went by, and Indie's Mummy's
tummy grew bigger

and bigger.

One day when Indie was eating her boiled egg and dippy soldiers, she asked her Mummy, "If we don't like this baby can we put it back?"

"No, silly," said her Mummy. "Besides, I **know** you'll like it, it will be a friend for you. A friend who will be with you for ever."

Indie turned her egg upside down and hit it with her spoon.

At the end of the summer, when the sandpit had been put away and all the leaves were falling off the trees, Indie's Mummy showed her the new bed.

Indie got in it one day — with the cat from next door.

Her Mummy said she'd rather she didn't do that any more, and bought her a toy crib for her doll Gus, but Gus didn't like it and went back to sleeping in Indie's bed.

"Wouldn't it be exciting if our baby was here in time for Christmas?" said Daddy when they were putting decorations on the Christmas tree.

"Will it try and open my stocking?" asked Indie.

"Of course not," said Daddy. "It'll be too little."

Indie stared at the fairy on top of the Christmas tree and made a wish.

Soon after Christmas Day when Father Christmas had been and Indie and Cleo had played with each other's presents, Daddy came rushing in and said, "I've got a great surprise for you."

Indie looked up from her painting, hoping it was a dog. "The baby has just come out of Mummy's tummy, and if you're very quiet we can go and have a look."

Indie looked at the baby.

"What do you think?" said her Mummy.
"Where's the rest of it?" asked Indie.

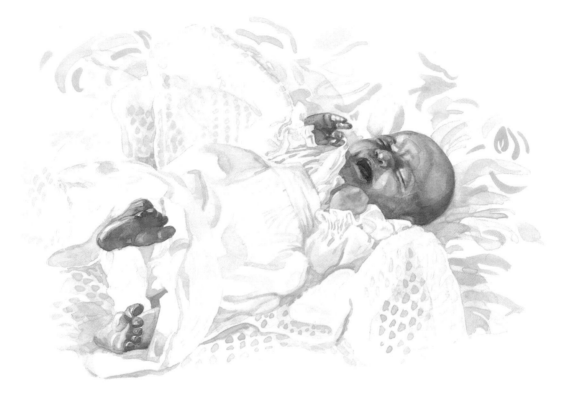

Her Mummy unwrapped the blanket and there was the baby — not much bigger than Indie's doll Gus.

"It's a little boy," said Mummy. "And we'll call him Archie. Archie, this is your sister India Rose."

"What's he like?" asked Cleo.

"Squashed up," said Indie. "All he does is drink milk from Mummy's bosom, and go to the loo."

"He sounds silly," said Cleo.

"He is," said Indie.

"When will he play with us?" asked Cleo.

"His feet have got to grow a bit first," said Indie.

All through the spring Archie was busy
growing. Sometimes Indie gave him a bottle, but
he was very squirmy. She tried to help bath
him, but he was very slippery.

In the summer Archie was given a teddy bear
that Indie liked a lot — so she took it
away from him.

"Now that's not very nice," said Daddy. "You
must always remember about sharing."

Indie wished some days that **she** was a baby.
In fact, some days she pretended she **was** a
baby — she spat her food out,

she wouldn't use her potty,
and
she cried when she went to bed.

"You're being a silly-billy," said her Mummy.
"I'm not," said Indie. "I want to be a baby."
"But you were a baby," said Mummy, "and now you're my special big girl – and Archie's the baby."

On the morning of Archie's first birthday Indie sat beside him, in her new party dress, for a photograph.

He had a cake with one candle.

"What do you think he'd like for his birthday? asked Mummy.

"He wants a dog," said Indie.

But he didn't get one, he got some bricks instead.

Soon Indie started going to Nursery School in the mornings. She went with her friend Cleo, and they did finger painting and singing and made things out of coloured paper. Indie could count up to 20.

"You can't do that, can you, Archie?" said Indie.

"Yes," said Archie.

"Don't be silly," said Indie.

When Indie came home from school, Archie would get very excited and dribble and try to walk and fall down a lot. He would shout "Nindy."

Sometimes he'd been playing with Indie's toys while she'd been at school.

"Bad boy, Archie," she'd say, and one day she gave him a pinch.

Big tears fell out of his eyes, and he started to cry.

Indie's Mummy shouted from the kitchen, "What's going on?"

"Nothing," shouted Indie.

"Why did you do it?" asked Cleo.

"I don't know," said Indie.

When Archie could walk he wanted to go everywhere with Indie. Sometimes she'd let him, and sometimes she wouldn't.

They slept in the same room now, and in the morning Indie would look out of her bed and see Archie, and Archie would look out of his cot and see Indie

One day Archie started playing
with Gus, so

Indie snatched Gus away –

Archie snatched him back,
and then Indie pushed Archie,
and Archie pushed Indie.

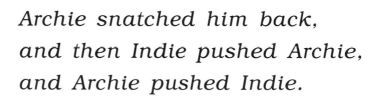

"It's mine," shouted Indie.
"It's mine," shouted Archie.
He'd learned to talk now.

In November Indie had a bad cold. Her head felt hot and her nose felt stuffy. She had to stay in bed.

Archie came and sat beside her. He brought her all his books, his new car and his favourite Teddy.

When she was better, Mummy took Indie and Archie to the playground for a treat. Lots of children were there — Cleo was on the swings and another girl called Lucy was on the slide. Archie loved the slide.

Suddenly Indie saw Lucy push Archie over.

"It's **my** slide," she was shouting. "You can't have a turn."

When Indie saw Lucy push Archie again she rushed over to his side. She helped him up – his knee was bleeding but he was being very brave. Indie put her arm round him.

"He's only little – don't you ever do that again," she said.

"Why not?" said Lucy.

Because he's my brother, and I love him, and I won't let anybody hurt him."

On the day that school finished for the
Christmas holidays Indie and Cleo were sitting
on the steps eating a peanut butter sandwich.

"I'm getting a dog for Christmas," said Cleo.

"Oh," said Indie, taking a big bite.

"Will you be sad you haven't got one?" said
Cleo.

Indie thought. "Oh, no," she said. "I'd much rather have a brother."

And she meant it.